S0-AYQ-384

Back to Nature

Don't miss the other Invincible Girls Club adventures!

Home Sweet Forever Home
Art with Heart

THE INVINCIBLE GIRLS CLUB

BOOK 3

BACK TO NATURE

by Rachele Alpine
illustrated by Addy Rivera Sonda

Aladdin
New York   London   Toronto   Sydney   New Delhi

This book is a work of fiction. Any references to historical events, real people, or real places are used fictitiously. Other names, characters, places, and events are products of the author's imagination, and any resemblance to actual events or places or persons, living or dead, is entirely coincidental.

ALADDIN
An imprint of Simon & Schuster Children's Publishing Division
1230 Avenue of the Americas, New York, New York 10020
First Aladdin hardcover edition November 2021
Text copyright © 2021 by Rachele Alpine
Illustrations copyright © 2021 by Addy Rivera Sonda
Also available in an Aladdin paperback edition.
All rights reserved, including the right of reproduction in whole or in part in any form.
ALADDIN and related logo are registered trademarks of Simon & Schuster, Inc.
For information about special discounts for bulk purchases, please contact Simon & Schuster Special Sales at 1-866-506-1949 or business@simonandschuster.com.
The Simon & Schuster Speakers Bureau can bring authors to your live event. For more information or to book an event contact the Simon & Schuster Speakers Bureau at 1-866-248-3049 or visit our website at www.simonspeakers.com.
Book designed by Heather Palisi
The illustrations for this book were rendered digitally.
The text of this book was set in Celeste.
Manufactured in the United States of America 1021 FFG
2 4 6 8 10 9 7 5 3 1
Library of Congress Control Number 2021936035
ISBN 9781534475397 (hc)
ISBN 9781534475380 (pbk)
ISBN 9781534475403 (ebook)

For Camp Christopher . . .
I want to linger, a little longer, a little longer here with you.
And as the years go by, I'll think of you and sigh,
my camping days at Christopher.

Of all the things I'd been skeptical about,
I didn't feel skeptical about this: the
wilderness had a clarity that included me.
-Cheryl Strayed

Contents

A TREE-MENDOUS MESS

There was a colossal bang from above.

A shake-the-room kind of bang.

A sonic boom kind of bang.

"What in the world was that?" I asked Grammy. The two of us were in her family room watching TV and knitting. We did it every night: our special Ruby and Grammy time. My parents owned a two-family house, and we lived on the top floor while Grammy lived below. It was the perfect setup because it meant unlimited time with her; all I had to do was walk down a flight of steps!

"I think an elephant is bowling up there," she said.

"Or there's a bunch of hippos jumping rope," I joked.

"Now, that would be something I'd like to see!" she said.

"Whatever is going on, I'm glad I'm here and not up there. Dad versus the baby furniture will not end well."

"You've got that right," Grammy said. "I'm not a betting woman, but if I were, my money would be on the furniture."

An item clattered onto the floor above us, and Dad yelled something we couldn't make out.

Grammy picked up her knitting and pointed at mine with one of her needles. "Just keep knitting," she said, which was our mantra when anything around us was not exactly going as planned.

Which didn't happen often because agendas and lists were my jam. I even had scheduled time to work on my weekly schedule, because I made it a priority to ensure that life ran smoothly.

That's probably why I loved knitting. If you followed the pattern, whatever you made came out exactly as it should. Knitting was predictable. And nothing could relax me the way the *click, click, click* of the needles did.

I settled back into the familiar rhythm of adding new stitches and focused on the TV. A man and woman had entered the kitchen of an enormous house, and the woman complained that it was too small.

"Um, that kitchen is almost bigger than our entire house," I said. "How in the world does she think that's small?"

"She hates it," Grammy said. "She's going to pick the first one."

"Do you think so? Her husband was into the house with the swimming pool."

The two of us went back and forth, commenting on the houses and making guesses about which one the couple would choose. This was our thing. Watching house-hunting shows while knitting. The perfect way to spend an evening!

The couple had toured the houses and I had finished five rows on my scarf when another giant boom from above startled me.

Dad yelled, and this time there was no mistaking his frustration.

"Just keep knitting, keep knitting," I said, and aggressively stabbed at my yarn with the needle.

"How much more do you have to go?"

"Almost done," I said, and held my scarf up.

"It's gorgeous," Grammy replied. "Your best one yet!"

"You say that about all my scarves," I said, and laughed.

"It's true! Each one gets better and better! Maybe after you finish this one, you'll knit a blanket for the baby!"

My good mood shifted at the mention of the baby.

"Yeah, maybe," I said as I played with a red piece of yarn hanging off the scarf.

The baby.

Or more specifically, my new baby sibling.

Of course I was excited about being a big sister, but the baby was all anyone talked about. New baby, baby, baby. All. The. Time. My family acted as if this were the first baby ever born in the history of the world. And the baby wasn't even here yet. If my parents gave this much attention to it now, how much worse would things be when the baby was finally here?

That was something I didn't want to think about. Every time I did, my insides turned shaky, like I was on a boat that was rocking in the waves.

"I'm not even sure this baby is going to get a crib to put a blanket in," I said instead as a series of booms interrupted my thoughts.

Grammy chuckled. "You might be right about that."

The two of us settled in to watch more TV, knit, and try to ignore the thumps above us.

A new couple on the TV was about to reveal their house choice when Grammy yawned. And since yawns were super contagious between the two of us, it soon became a yawn fest!

"We're two sleepyheads," Grammy said.

"You've got that right." I looked at the clock on the wall. "I'd better head upstairs. Although, I'm not sure how I'll sleep with that racket."

I finished the row I'd been knitting and tucked everything into my bag. It was an old backpack of Mom's that she'd passed on to me. It was big enough to hold my knitting, her old phone that I used to take pictures and write notes in, my journal, and whatever book I was reading. The perfect bag for a reporter/knitter/lover of words.

"Be safe up there," Grammy joked as she

hugged me, her scent of roses and baby powder settling over me like a blanket.

"I'll try," I said as I stepped into the hallway. I yawned again and made my way up the steps, giggling to myself. I really had a bad case of the yawns. My warm, comfy bed sounded wonderful, and I couldn't wait to dive under the sheets and snuggle into a deep, wonderful sleep.

I opened my front door to darkness, which was odd. Mom and Dad always left the light on for me when I was downstairs.

"Ouch!" I yelled out as my knee bumped into something huge and solid. "What in the world?"

I switched on the light just as Dad stuck his head out my bedroom door.

"Hi, Bee," he shouted down the hall, using his silly nickname for me. When I was little, he called me his Bumble Bee instead of Ruby. Somewhere along the way, it got shortened to Bee, which was pretty much all he called me now. "Sorry about the mess. Your mom and I got wrapped up in what we were doing and lost track of time."

"A mess?" I asked as I swept my hand around the room, which was filled with boxes, packing paper, tape, tools, and various baby-related items. "I'm not sure I'd call this a mess. More like a colossal hurricane of destruction."

"It's a bit much, isn't it?" he asked sheepishly.

"It doesn't matter. I'm exhausted," I said. "I'm planning to go to sleep."

Dad glanced toward my room. It was quick, but I caught it.

"Is that okay?" I asked, and looked at him suspiciously.

He ran his hand through his hair and stalled. A telltale sign that something was up.

"How about a late-night snack first?" he asked.

"I'm really tired," I told him. "Sleep is all I want right now."

"Okay, well, about your room—" he started, but I didn't let him finish.

I pushed past him to the open door.

I wished I hadn't.

Our family room was nothing compared to the shape my room was in. Correction. The room I would soon share with my new brother or sister.

"What did you do in here?" I took in the empty boxes, packaging material, tools, pieces of paper, and the pieces of a crib and changing station. Mom sat in the middle of it, exhausted. Her hair was in a messy bun, and she let out a breath so big that it blew her bangs up into the air.

"Honey, I'm sorry," she said. "We'll clear this out. It turns out, putting together a crib and changing station is a bit harder than we thought."

"I'll say," I said as I thought about how nice and neat I kept my room. Everything had a place and everything stayed in that place.

"I guess when the instructions tell you to go step-by-step, it's for a reason. It's not a good idea to go rogue and try to figure it out yourself," Dad said.

"I could have told you that," I said.

"I tried to," Mom pointed out.

"It's under control," Dad said. "I'll clean every-thing up quickly."

But there was nothing quick about what was all over my bedroom floor.

"Can it wait until the morning? Since my bed is free, I'd rather go to sleep."

"Sure, Bee," Dad said. "I promise that by the time you get home from school tomorrow, these boxes and tools will all be gone."

I gave Dad a weak smile and thought about how this wasn't about the chaos on the floor. The truth was that my room would never be the same. They might be able to clean up the mess, but they couldn't clean up the amount of attention a baby needed and how my new little brother or sister would soon take over a space that had always been just for me.

2 AN UNBE-LEAF-ABLE IDEA

Breaking news.

The next morning wasn't any better.

It was worse.

My bedroom door flew open and Dad burst in.

"Rise and shine!" he said in a voice that was a million times more energized than how I felt. "Wakey, wakey!"

I groaned and threw my pillow at him.

"Why are you in here so early?"

"Early?" Dad asked. "Bee, it's late. You're going to miss the bus if you don't get moving."

"Wait, what?" I sat up and rubbed my eyes. My alarm clock sat on the dresser, the screen dark. As in, it wasn't even on. "What happened to my clock?"

Dad gave me a guilty look as it dawned on him. "Shoot, I unplugged it last night. We needed to charge the drill. I guess I forgot to plug it back in."

"Dad!" I said, and groaned again. "What time is it?"

He checked his phone. "Seven ten."

"Seven ten!" I repeated in a panic. "I can't believe you let me sleep this late! I'm not even going to have time for a shower or breakfast. Can you drive me?"

"Sorry, Bee, not today. Your mom has an early-morning doctor's appointment," he said. The uneven feeling inside me came back. Dad was always okay with driving me to school, especially when there was time to stop at the doughnut shop a few blocks away. At least he used to be.

"Don't look so worried. You'll be fine. You've got fifteen minutes until the bus comes. Get dressed, brush your teeth, and I'll toast a bagel that you can eat on the road."

"You make it sound so simple," I muttered.

"Embrace the chaos," Dad said. "And look on the bright side. Once the baby comes, none of us will need an alarm clock."

"That doesn't make me feel any better," I grumbled. The idea of a crying baby waking me up had no bright side to it.

After Dad left my room, I forced myself out of bed. If this had been a regular school morning, I'd have woken to the alarm on my radio and spent time writing in my journal before I got out of bed. Then I'd have taken a quick shower and joined Grammy for breakfast, where we started the day knitting one row on our current WIP, which was knitter-speak for "Work in Progress."

I had a whole morning routine to ease into my day, but today there was no easing. Instead I was thrown headfirst into it.

"Up and at 'em," I mumbled, because there'd be no rising and shining today. I swung my legs over the edge of my bed and stood up.

"Ow!" I yelled as my bare foot landed on something sharp and pointy. I jumped back in pain, only to bump into a bunch of cardboard boxes. My arms flailed around like windmills for a moment before I lost my balance and went crashing to the floor.

"You have to be kidding me," I said, and rubbed my sore foot.

I carefully made my way across my bedroom, avoiding any of the stuff my parents had left on the floor.

Things weren't any better in the hallway. More boxes sat against the wall, so I had to dodge my way around them. An obstacle course in my own house.

"How much stuff does a baby even need?" I asked out loud. "Doesn't a baby just eat, sleep, and poop?"

I brushed my teeth, splashed water onto my face, and ran a comb through my hair before pulling it into a ponytail. I could practically hear an invisible clock in my head ticking down the minutes until the bus came.

I rushed back to my room to change and bumped into one of the boxes along the way.

"Augh!" I yelled, and slammed the door to make my point. However, the joke was on me. My parents had lined up the pieces of the crib against the wall, and as the door closed, they clattered down into a big pile covering what little space had been left on my bedroom floor.

"I give up!" I shouted.

Somehow I made it to the bus in time, but that wasn't nearly enough to help my bad mood. My friends could tell something was up the second I stormed into our classroom and dumped my unorganized mess of stuff onto the floor.

"Whoa, Ruby, you do not look like you had a good morning," Lauren said, eyeing my wrinkled outfit and messy hair.

"Is everything okay?" Myka asked.

"Yeah, what's going on?" Emelyn added.

"Everything," I said in a super-dramatic way. "Especially the new baby."

"I thought you were excited to be a big sister," Myka said.

"I *was*. Emphasis on the word 'was.' The baby isn't even here yet and it's taking over our entire house. We have so much stuff. I'm afraid I'm going to be buried alive. And it's driving me up the wall."

"I know what that's like," Myka said in solidarity. "Whenever my brothers and I get home in the evening, our mudroom is full of our backpacks, shoes, sports gear, instruments, and a million other random things that make it impossible to walk in there."

"At least you have a mudroom and your own room," I said. "My parents told me the other day that since we don't have a third bedroom, I have to share my room with the baby. Someone I haven't even met. A complete stranger! Is that even allowed? What if we don't get along?"

My mind whirled with the possibilities of what could go wrong once the baby invaded my room. My thoughts then moved on to the baby invading my life and my relationship with my parents. Everything was changing so fast; I wasn't sure I could keep up.

"I don't know what to do," I told my friends. "It seems as if things are going from bad to worse, and I have no idea how to stop it."

"This sounds like a problem for our club," Myka said.

"Can the Invincible Girls help?" I asked.

"Can we help?" Myka said as if that were the most outrageous question in the world.

"Helping is what we do!" Emelyn added.

"I know, but our club's mission is to help change the world. Does it work when we're only focused on one person?" I asked.

"Of course it does," Emelyn said. "One less problem for one person means one more piece of happiness in the world. Imagine if we could do that for everyone!"

"Yep," Myka agreed. "Just like when I play

soccer. When my team helps one of us become a better kicker or faster runner, it helps all of us play better."

"Makes complete sense," I said, and gave them a thumbs-up. "It's totally okay to focus on one person in our quest to change the world."

"Yep, and that person is you!" Myka said. "So what is the true problem?"

My friends leaned toward me, ready to spring into action, which made my bad mood evaporate. There was nothing greater than having people on your side.

"Let's get planning!" I declared as I pulled out my notebook. The one I scheduled and listed and plotted in. I opened to a new page, wrote the word "PROBLEM" at the top, and then hesitated.

Should I tell them the truth? I wondered. That I worried my parents might get so busy with the baby, they'd forget about me? This might have been something I'd been thinking about a lot, but those words were scary to say out loud. I held my pen over the page, unsure of what to do.

"Remember, we're here to help," Emelyn said gently, and the other two nodded in agreement.

"Okay," I said. I lowered the pen tip to the paper and wrote, *My parents are forgetting me.*

I dropped my pen like it was on fire. Somehow, writing it down had made it a million times more real.

"Forgetting you?" Lauren asked. "What do you mean?"

"The baby," I said. "It's changing everything. I swear I could stay at one of your houses for a week and they wouldn't even notice."

"They have too much on their minds, trying to get everything ready," Emelyn reasoned.

"Exactly," I replied. "They have *so much* on their minds that those thoughts have pushed aside anything else. Including me. We haven't spent time together in forever, and I miss them."

"I get what you're saying." Myka chewed on her bottom lip and studied me. She nodded slowly. "When your mom drove us to the library last week, all she talked about was baby stuff."

"Yes!" I said. "And that was even after we told her about our science project. If a super-awesome science project can't get their attention, what can?"

"I promise we aren't going to forget you," Lauren said, and draped her arm around my shoulders.

"Nope, never!" Myka agreed, and their pledge of eternal friendship helped.

"You couldn't if you tried," I joked, and then sighed. "I just wish my parents would take a break from the baby stuff."

"What if you took a trip somewhere? You know, to get away from it all, have some family time, and relax?" Myka suggested.

"Ohhhh! Like Disney! Or a tropical island!" Lauren said excitedly. "And I could come too!"

"Pretty sure my mom isn't going to want to

fly somewhere. Not when she's so close to having the baby."

"What about a hotel with a pool for a night or two?" Emelyn suggested. "My cousins do that once in a while."

"Hmmm," I said as I considered it. "I like the pool part, but the three of us in a tiny hotel room sounds more crowded than our house."

"Whenever I need a break from my brothers, I like to go into our backyard," Myka said. "It's quiet and open and—"

"Wait! That's it!" I interrupted. "We need to get back to nature!"

"Back to nature?" Emelyn asked.

"Yes!" I said, my excitement building. I couldn't believe I hadn't thought of this before. My idea was brilliant. It was perfect. It was precisely what we needed. "We are going camping!"

"We?" Emelyn asked.

"Yep, all four of us and my parents!" I confirmed.

"Won't we take away from you spending time with your parents?" Emelyn replied.

"You're my best friends," I said to them. "I can't be away from the three of you for that long. Besides, we've all been busy lately. It will be a weekend for us to bond!"

"Can't we bond here? Do we really need to go camping?" Emelyn said, not exactly sharing my enthusiasm.

"Nope, we totally need to go," I told her. "Think about it . . . nothing but trees, fresh air, the sounds of nature surrounding us. In other words, no TVs, computers, or phones. Instead tons of hiking, s'mores, and just hanging out with each other! In real life!"

"No electronics?" Lauren asked. "That's like living in old-fashioned times!"

"I'm sure you can handle it for a few days. It's not the end of the world," I teased. "Trust me, it's going to be incredible."

"You say that as if we're already planning to go," Emelyn said.

"Because we are! Come on, I thought you wanted to help me," I begged.

"I'm in!" Myka said. "It sounds like a blast."

I clapped my hands together. "Great! Emelyn? Lauren? Please, pretty please?"

Lauren nodded. "Okay, sure. My stepdad is always talking about taking us camping. Might as well get a head start!"

And once Emelyn saw Lauren agree, she nodded too.

"I don't want to be left behind," Emelyn said.

"Then it's settled!" I said with a grin. "The Invincible Girls are about to take on the great outdoors for some bonding!"

TAKE A HIKE

3

"Stress no more. I have found a solution to our problem," I announced to my parents when I got home from school.

"Problem?" Mom asked. She sat on the couch and paged through a magazine, with her feet propped up on one of the endless boxes we had. A plate of cookies rested on her giant stomach, and although it looked funny, I had to admit it was practical.

"Our problem," I repeated. "The fact that this baby is taking over our lives."

"Interesting," Mom said. "I wasn't aware of this problem."

"How could you not notice it?" I swept my hand across the room. "First of all, we don't have any room anywhere because our house is a cluttered mess."

"Hey, your mom has a new footstool!" Dad said as he winked at me. "But you're right, this place is a bit crowded at the moment for three people."

"Four," Mom reminded us as she placed her hand on her belly.

"Exactly!" I said. "And second, the baby is all you talk about. Everything is baby, baby, baby. When was the last time the three of us spent quality time together?"

"We eat dinner together every night," Dad said.

"And the favorite topic at the dinner table is

the baby," I said. "What we need is to take a break."

"A break?" Mom asked.

"Yep, we need to head to the woods to get away from it all," I declared.

"Whoa, that escalated fast. We went from a messy house full of baby stuff to running away into the woods," Dad said. "Did I miss a step in there?"

"Camping in the woods," I corrected him. "A weekend of family time. Wouldn't that be great? We can disconnect and spend tons of time together as we become one with nature. Live off the land and experience the magnificent splendor of Mother Nature."

Mom laughed so hard, she snorted. "Ruby, I had no idea you were so into roughing it in the woods."

"I'm into us," I corrected her. "Our family spending time together. Camping and having fun."

"I love you, sweetie, but 'fun' isn't the word I'd

use to describe a weekend camping when I'm six months pregnant."

"You might not be into it," Dad said to Mom, "but I think it's a wonderful idea, Bee! I used to camp when I was younger."

"You did?" I asked.

"I sure did! Fishing, canoeing, hiking, campfires, those were some of my favorite times as a kid."

"So we can go?" I asked.

"The two of you can go," Mom said. "By all means, have fun, but I'll hold down the fort here."

"Let me check into it and see if I can find an open campsite. I'd love to take you," Dad added.

Mom must have seen the disappointment on my face. "Ruby, we can plan some bonding time together too. In fact, if you want to get the calendar, we can pencil in a few Mom-Ruby dates and a few as a family."

"I'm always up for family dates," Dad said.

"And a camping weekend with just the two of us sounds awesome too."

"Do you know what would be even more awesome?" I asked.

"I'm afraid to ask," Dad joked.

"A camping weekend with the rest of the Invincible Girls!" I said.

Dad laughed. "Were they part of the plan all along?"

"Maybe," I said in a way that let him know that was totally the plan.

"All right, then! How could we not invite them? If their parents are okay with it, the more the merrier!"

"Woo-hoo!" I jumped in the air with excitement. I landed on the corner of one of the boxes, and it poked into my side. I rubbed the sore spot and turned back to my parents. "We desperately need to get out of here and into some wide-open space."

"The only great outdoors I'll be visiting is the

ice cream store with the walk-up window," Mom joked.

"Are you sure?" I tried to convince her one last time.

"I can get you the finest blow-up mattress that money can buy," Dad added.

"Nope, nope, and in case you didn't hear me, nope," she said, and put her arms behind her to rest her head on. "I plan to relax and enjoy the peace and quiet."

There was a small tug of disappointment inside me. The weekend was supposed to include Mom too, but I told myself to look on the bright side. A weekend with Dad and my friends would also be special.

"I'll clean up the house before we leave, so you can have the weekend to do absolutely nothing and we can come back to a house baby-clutter-free," Dad said.

I eyed the stacks of magazines, the little bowls of candy he had stashed everywhere, mugs,

mismatched socks, papers from work, and Mom's crossword puzzle books. "I'm pretty sure tidying up isn't going to fix this place," I said.

Dad held up my knitting backpack, which was full of my latest project and skeins of yarn. "I'm pretty sure your mom and I aren't the knitters around here."

"Oh, come on, that's the only thing of mine sitting around," I argued.

Dad raised his eyebrow. "Is that so? Then your piece of the apple pie cooling in the kitchen right now is mine, since you're not staking claim to it."

"That's not what I meant!" I protested.

"Actually, I made the pie, so technically it's mine," Mom said as she pulled herself up with a big *oomph* and rubbed her stomach. "But I'll be nice and share. Ruby, how about you go get Grammy, your dad can look into taking you camping, and I'll dream about a house entirely to myself?"

"Be careful what you wish for," I told Mom.

"We might end up moving into the woods and living there."

"I'm not complaining. With the two of you living in the woods, that means more pie for me! Now go get Grammy. I'm starving," Mom said, and playfully pushed me toward the door.

I hurried downstairs, excited to tell her about our camping adventure.

THE INVINCIBLE GIRLS BRANCH OUT

4

My life at home might have been a disorganized mess, but the plans for the camping trip came together so easily that it was as if it was meant to be.

Dad reserved a campsite at Butler Woods, and two weeks later, the wilderness called and we answered. He borrowed two tents from a friend, took me shopping for supplies, and talked to Myka's, Lauren's, and Emelyn's parents.

"I'm calling it. This is the official start to our adventure!" Dad announced as he pulled onto the highway.

I held up one of my knitting needles in salute. "Here's to adventuring in the wild!"

My friends cheered in response, and I could not wait to get there. This was it. We were going to have an incredible weekend!

I pulled my notebook from my bag and flipped to my plans and lists for the weekend. I'd spent all week creating them, to make sure it would be the most epic weekend ever.

It might sound strange, but I liked thinking about what could go wrong and then solving the problem. A well-executed plan meant my world ran smoothly, and when my world ran smoothly, I was a very happy person.

"We'll be pulling into Butler Woods in one hour and twenty-three minutes," I told the group.

"Wow, that's extremely exact," Lauren said.

I gave her a knowing smile. "Punctuality is my expertise, and when you know, you know. A good reporter never reveals her sources."

"Except when your source is the GPS on your dad's phone." Emelyn pointed to the map on the screen.

"We now have one hour and twenty-two minutes," I told the group, ignoring Emelyn's comment. "We'd better go over the itinerary for the weekend and some rules."

"I thought the whole idea of this weekend was to relax and spend time together," Myka said. "Don't a schedule and rules go against that?"

"Not at all. I created them to make sure that we *could* relax. They're going to help us not worry about a thing," I told my friends, but they didn't look convinced. "All right, let's start with the rules. These are important. I did some research about camping etiquette. These are super official and created by the American Camping Association. So technically they're not my rules but the people in charge of camping."

"There are people in charge of camping?" Lauren asked, an eyebrow raised.

"Of course," I said.

"And thank goodness for that," Dad chimed in. "Without people in charge, it would be camping chaos! Imagine it . . . marshmallows being roasted on the wrong sticks, mosquitoes not knowing who to bite, trees falling in the woods with no one to hear them."

"Dad," I said. "This isn't a joke. We need to take this seriously. Which means, rule number one . . . Leave everything as you found it. In other words, look with your eyes and not your hands. We are the guests in the woods, and we need to give the earth the respect it deserves."

Emelyn and Lauren giggled. I brushed their laughs off and continued, "So we can't pick up things or mess with stuff in the woods. Also, we can never leave a campfire unattended. That's how disaster happens."

"I'll take care of that one," Dad said. "Just call me the fire master. I'm a pro on the grill and can't wait to show off my campfire skills!"

"And we'll eat good this weekend!" I announced. "I found a bunch of recipes on a blog about cooking outdoors."

Dad caught my eye in the rearview mirror and smiled. "I like the sound of that! We'll make a great team."

A great team, I thought, and grinned back at him. I'd have his attention on me and not on everything that needed to get done for the new baby. Just time spent with Dad.

"We also need to remember that it's not only nature we have to respect when camping but our neighbors and the campground. Keep things clean and our volume down," I told everyone.

"You girls keep your volume down?" Dad joked. "We might as well turn around now; that will never happen."

"We can be very quiet," Lauren said, and paused. "When we're sleeping!"

"Speaking of sleeping," I said. "Our schedule for tonight calls for an early bedtime. Of course, we can have a campfire and make s'mores, but we can't stay up super late because tomorrow we're getting up early to watch the sunrise!"

Watching the sun come up seemed like the perfect way to start a new day. I'd never done it before, and I was ridiculously excited about it.

"You want us to wake up before the sun?" Myka asked.

"Yeah, that's how it works," I told her. "We get up to see the sun come up."

"I'm tired already, thinking about it," Emelyn joked.

"It will be fun," I promised, but no one seemed convinced.

"Since we're talking rules, I have a few of my own we need to go over," Dad said.

"You too?" Lauren asked. "Wow, you and Ruby really are alike!"

Dad chuckled. "Yep! Especially with how neat we are!"

I shot Dad a look. "Oh please! The word 'neat' has never been used with you before. And what rules? You know I like to prepare for anything and everything."

"That's why I didn't mention it," Dad said. "I wanted the weekend to be relax-city."

"Planning is how I relax," I reminded Dad.

"That, Bee, is not how a person relaxes," Dad said. "Now back to the important stuff. There isn't a lot, but I do want to make sure we have fun *and* stay safe. So first, always use the buddy system. All the time. No exceptions. Everywhere you go."

"Even the bathroom?" Lauren joked.

"Yep, even the bathroom," Dad confirmed.

"Bathroom buddies, got it. What else?" I asked, irritated that he hadn't told me these rules ahead of time.

"Fire safety," he said. "I'm glad you mentioned not leaving it unattended. That's a very important detail. You also want to make sure not to run around it or throw things into it."

"Don't worry, you can trust us," Myka promised. "My family loves to sit around our fire pit. I know how to be careful around it."

"Perfect," Dad said. "Now, the most important rule is to never, ever leave any food out. Not just outside but also in the tents or your backpacks. It gets put in the trunk of the car or the canister I got that we keep in the tree."

"Why would we keep food in a tree?" I asked.

"So the bears can't get to it," Dad said as if it were obvious. Which, it wasn't. That was a fact I would never, ever have overlooked.

"Ha ha, Dad," I said. He loved to throw some pretend obstacle into my plans. He said it built character to be able to pivot and turn, but I never fell for it.

"Sorry, sweetie, but this time I'm not joking. Bears while camping are a serious thing."

Emelyn turned to me with wide eyes. "You're taking us into woods full of bears?"

"I didn't know anything about this," I said, my voice as panicked as Emelyn's.

"The woods are not full of bears," Dad corrected her. "It's nothing to worry about as long as we take precautions. They want to avoid us as much as we want to avoid them. Well, unless you leave a tasty treat out, and then they'll come running."

"Not funny," I said. It wasn't funny at all.

I thought about the research, lists, and preparation I had done. Not ever had the thought that we'd be heading into woods full of bears cross my mind.

Nope, a bear attack was most definitely not on the schedule.

A BIT OF TENT-SION

My mind spun with worst-case scenarios about bears, and none of them were good.

But thoughts of bears were pushed aside once Dad pulled into Butler Woods. As soon as I saw the thick woods and signs marking the start of trails, I had no doubt that this was the best decision ever.

"Can you smell it?" I asked after we climbed out of the SUV.

"Smell what?" Lauren asked, and took a deep breath.

I spread my arms wide and spun around. "The fresh air! It's invigorating!"

"Invigorating?" Lauren asked. "Definition, please."

"It means 'energizing.' Something that makes you feel awake and happy," I said. I loved learning new words and didn't mind explaining them to my friends when they asked.

"It is pretty great," Myka agreed. "Not to mention the view. Nothing but trees and sky."

"I can sketch some amazing pictures here," Emelyn said in agreement.

I bumped her hip with mine. "And that's exactly what you should do. Art is one hundred percent part of a simple life."

Dad did a long stretch and took in our campsite.

"Home sweet home," he announced.

"Um, I'm not seeing much home here," Lauren commented as she walked around the space, which consisted of a lot of dirt, a fire pit, and a well-worn picnic table. "Where exactly is the bathroom?"

"This place is a bit . . . rustic," Dad admitted.

"How rustic?" Lauren asked.

"There should be an outhouse we share with a couple of other sites right beyond the trees over there," Dad said.

"An outhouse?" Lauren wrinkled her nose. "Who wants to come with me to our four-star restroom?"

"I'll go," Emelyn volunteered.

"And Dad, Myka, and I will work on setting up the campsite," I said, because that was the first step on my list of things to do once we'd arrived.

"Sounds like a plan," Dad said as he pulled out one of the tents we had packed. He spread everything out and examined it like a doctor who was about to perform a major surgery. "Hmmmm . . ."

He scratched his head and walked around in a slow circle.

"Is something wrong?" I asked, because according to my planning, nothing should go wrong.

"Maybe not . . . ," Dad said vaguely, and picked up a piece of the tent. "The instructions seem to be missing, but I'm sure we can figure this out."

He pulled out his phone.

"What are you doing?" I asked.

"Looking up instructions," he said, but I quickly shook my head.

"Nope, no can do. We're off the grid. No electronics, remember?"

"Bee, I don't have instructions," Dad protested.

"We don't need them," I said. "With two members of the Invincible Girls Club helping, we'll have these tents up in no time."

"No time" turned out to be almost an hour and a half, even with Emelyn and Lauren helping when they got back.

After what felt like forever, we finally figured out how to get the tents up and assembled. Dad waved his hands in front of our tent as if he were on a game show presenting a prize. "Behold, home sweet home for the next two nights! Why don't

49

you girls put your sleeping bags in your tent, and I'll get the fire started? I don't know about you, but I'm starving."

"Good plan," I said, and checked my watch and then my notebook. "We're twenty minutes behind schedule. We should be sitting down for dinner right now."

"Wait a minute," Lauren said, and narrowed her eyes. She put out her hand, palm up. "Hand it over."

"What?" I asked.

"Your watch."

I glanced down at my wrist. I had on a red digital watch Grammy had given me as a gift. It had been made to be worn all the time; it could even go in the water.

"No technology, remember?" Lauren added.

"A watch isn't technology," I argued.

"Sorry, kiddo. I'd say it is," Dad said. "Guess you'll have to use the sun."

Lauren wiggled her fingers at me. "Come on, give it up."

I reluctantly took the watch off and handed it to her. She walked to the SUV and put it in the glove compartment.

"There you go," she said. "Distraction gone."

"Let's get our stuff into the tent," Emelyn said before Lauren and I could argue anymore.

"Slumber party!" Myka cheered.

The four of us grabbed our stuff out of the trunk of Dad's SUV and moved it into our wilderness bedroom for the weekend.

"It's like we're camping by ourselves," I told my friends. Dad had agreed that the four of us could share a tent. We spread everything out inside the tent, and it was like one big cozy bed.

Emelyn lay down with her hands behind her head. "Now this is the life."

"I told you camping would be fun." I settled in next to her, and Myka and Lauren did the same.

Dad had left the rain cover off the top, so we could see the sky through the mesh. I couldn't wait to see the stars.

My stomach made a giant growling sound, and my friends laughed.

"Who needs a watch when you can use your stomach!" Myka said.

"I think it's time for dinner," Lauren confirmed.

"I think you're right," I agreed. "And wait until you see what I have planned!"

While writing and knitting were my true loves, cooking didn't come too far behind. It was another thing I shared with Grammy. If we weren't knitting, you'd better believe we were baking. Or more specifically, making something to snack on while we knitted.

I'd never cooked outside, though, so this was going to be an adventure. I'd spent a long time on the computer looking at different recipes that could be made around a campfire, and I couldn't wait to try out the ones I'd picked.

Tonight we'd feast on loaded baked potatoes, and if they tasted anywhere near as good as they looked in the pictures online, there wouldn't be anything left for the bears to get.

I showed everyone how to slice open a potato and add a bunch of toppings Mom had cut up and put into little containers. We wrapped the potatoes in foil, put them on the fire, and waited for perfection cooked over the open flame.

"Bon appétit!" I said as we dug into our dinner.

And perfection it was!

Somehow the campfire had made everything cheesy and crispy and delicious.

"Wow, if I'd known you could make vegetables taste this good, I'd have eaten them more often," Lauren joked, and she took a bite of potato with broccoli and bacon on it.

"Ditto. This might be the best thing I've ever had," Myka said as she picked up a piece of potato with a long string of cheese oozing out. "Why doesn't everyone make their potatoes on a fire?"

"Maybe that's the next Invincible Girls project," I said excitedly. "To open a campfire-baked-potato restaurant!"

Dad shook his head as he finished chewing his bite. "Whoa, slow down. Let's focus on this weekend first before we plan future adventures."

"I'm kidding," I told Dad, but then I turned to my friends and mouthed, *Let's do it!* The three of them nodded, and each gave me a thumbs-up, and I was sure that if this was something the Invincible Girls decided to do, we'd be brilliant at it.

We were almost done eating when the music started.

"Do you hear that?" I asked, and tilted my head to make sure I wasn't imagining things.

"It sounds like someone singing," Lauren said.

"More than one someone," Myka added. "And a guitar!"

We remained still as we listened.

"I like it. It's got a Beatles vibe to it," Dad said.

"A song about bugs?" I asked, and wrinkled my nose.

Dad clutched his heart in a joking way. "How does my daughter not know who the Beatles are? I've failed as a parent."

I rolled my eyes at Dad as Emelyn spoke up. "They were, like, the biggest and best band ever. My mom and I listen to them a lot."

Dad stood and bowed to Emelyn. "You, Miss Emelyn, are officially the coolest kid I've ever met."

"Hey!" I protested. "I listen to your country music!"

"True," Dad said. "But it's evident that we'll need to expand your music reach to make sure you know all the greats."

The song wasn't bad.

At least the first time.

Then they played it again.

And again.

After the third time, I turned to my friends, wide-eyed.

"That's the same song, right? That they keep playing."

"Same song," Myka agreed.

"Multiple times," Emelyn confirmed.

"A true one-hit wonder," Dad joked.

"The only thing I wonder," I said, "is when they'll play something else."

As the people launched into the song again, I decided we needed to focus on something else. A distraction from the song that never ended.

"I think it's time," I told the group.

"Time for what?" Lauren asked.

"S'mores!" I announced with a grin. "I'll grab the ingredients, and you three can get sticks for roasting marshmallows."

I headed to Dad's SUV, dug through one of the containers, and pulled out marshmallows and graham crackers but couldn't find the chocolate bars. Mom had bought twenty bars of chocolate. She'd thought it was a little excessive, but I'd told her that s'mores were an important part of camping and we didn't want to run out of ingredients.

But now we had run out before we had even started.

"They have to be in here," I muttered, and searched the container again. I vividly remembered them sitting on the kitchen counter. I had waited until the end to put them into the container, so they wouldn't get smooshed and broken by everything else.

"But I never put them in," I said slowly, as the realization sank in. I had forgotten the most important part of camping. How could I have done that?

I trudged back to the group, disappointed in myself.

"I have some bad news," I announced. "I forgot something super important."

"What are you talking about?" Lauren asked.

"I'm sure that whatever you forgot isn't a big deal," Emelyn said.

"Well, it kind of is," I said, and cringed. "I left the chocolate bars at home."

"That's it?" Emelyn asked. "You made it sound as if you'd forgotten something major."

"But what's s'mores without chocolate?" I asked.

"Something totally different that we'll invent!" said Myka. "We're the Invincible Girls. We're not about to let some missing chocolate stop us!"

"Yes!" Lauren agreed. "No big deal. It's the marshmallows that I'm after; the more burnt, the better. So hand them over and let's get roasting!"

I laughed, relieved. "I can do that. The good news is that I brought tons of bags."

"Perfect!" Emelyn said, and pointed her stick at me. "Remember, don't sweat the small stuff. This is nothing to worry about."

"She's right," Dad said. "Graham crackers and marshmallows sound delicious."

"Thanks," I said. I was bummed about my mistake, but glad that my friends didn't look at it as one. With another major disaster averted, we could enjoy the night.

My friends and I laughed, joked, and told stories around the fire. We roasted an entire bag of marshmallows, and when we couldn't take

any more of their sweetness, we moved on to the graham crackers. And the girls were right, it worked out in the end.

Until the music started back up.

Or, more precisely, the one song started up again.

"They really do like that song," Myka said. "Like, *really* like it."

"I know that the whole idea of this trip was to get away from technology," I said. "But right now I'd give anything for a pair of noise-canceling headphones to drown out that song."

But I wasn't even sure a pair of headphones could block out the song, which went on and on and on.

AN UN-BEAR-ABLE INCIDENT

"**R**uby," a voice whispered late that night.

I opened my eyes, but it was too dark to see anything.

"Ruby," the voice whispered again, closer to me.

Was it a ghost?

Would a ghost know my name?

Probably not, but I wasn't taking any chances.

I stayed still so it looked like I was asleep.

This is a dream, this is a dream, this is a dream, I repeated in my head.

I had almost convinced myself it was, when the ghost grabbed my foot.

"Augh!" I yelled, but a hand clamped over my mouth.

"Shhh, Ruby. It's me. Myka."

I opened one of my eyes. "Myka?"

"Yeah, silly. What did you think I was, a ghost?" She laughed to herself, and I decided not to tell her that that was exactly what I'd thought she was. "I need to go to the bathroom."

"What time is it?" I asked.

"I don't know. . . . Late? Super late, but I really have to go."

"You can't go by yourself?" I asked, because my sleeping bag was so warm and comfy, and now that I knew Myka wasn't a ghost, all I wanted to do was close my eyes and drift back into a dream.

"Um, would you?"

Yeah, nope. She had a point.

"Please," she said. "Remember, your dad said

62

we had to use the buddy system this weekend. No matter what."

She had me there. We had promised Dad. I sighed and crawled out of my sleeping bag.

"Let me get my shoes on," I said.

I grabbed the flashlight next to my sleeping bag, and the two of us slipped out of the tent, careful not to wake up Lauren and Emelyn.

The air was chilly but smelled fresh and full of pine.

We walked for to the outhouse in silence, listening to the sounds of the night bugs. It was neat to be up so late. There was something special about being the only ones awake.

We were almost back to the tents when I glanced upward. I gasped.

"What is it?" Myka asked.

I pointed, not wanting to break the magic that swirled around me.

"It's beautiful!" Myka said as she tilted her head to the sky.

Above us millions of stars sparkled.

"It's like someone took fairy lights and hung them all over," Myka said, which was the perfect description.

"This is why people camp," I whispered. "You'd never see anything like this at home."

"It would be impossible to count them all," she said. "They're everywhere."

I slowly turned in a circle. Wispy clouds moved across the sky. It was quiet.

So quiet.

As if the entire world were asleep.

The calm of everything around me was exactly what I had been looking for when I'd suggested we get away.

My body had relaxed into a total state of peace. I was hypnotized by the stars, the fresh air, and the rustling of the night.

Wait. Rustling?

My body stiffened as I heard it again.

A rustling in the woods.

A *loud* rustling in the woods.

A rustling that was made by something that was not worried about keeping quiet as it plowed through the trees, leaves and sticks crunching under it.

Something that might possibly be a bear.

"Um, Myka, did you hear that?" I whispered to her.

"Hear what?" she asked.

"Shh!" I told her, my finger to my lips. "Don't say a word. This is important. Quite possibly life-and-death important."

But it was too late. Whatever it was barreled out of the trees and went straight to the picnic table. Soon there was a snorting noise and the sound of paper crinkling.

"The graham crackers!" I said as realization dawned. We must have left some of them out. An invitation for a bear to come to our campsite and have a midnight snack.

I thought about Dad's rule, and panic set in.

We were going to get eaten by a bear, and it was my fault!

"Don't move," I told her. "I'm pretty sure that's a bear."

"A bear?" Myka asked, her eyes wide. "What should we do?"

"I was going to ask you the same thing," I said.

What do you even do when there's a bear? I wondered. *Run? Play dead?* In all my careful planning, that was something I'd never imagined. I wasn't prepared, and now we might end up as bear food. I had no clue, and I really didn't want to find out. I wished I'd asked Dad more about the bears when he had mentioned them.

"What if it goes after everyone in the tents?" Myka asked.

"Don't say that," I said, because it was something I hadn't thought about, and now it was added to my list of fears. My endless list of fears at the moment.

Myka gripped my upper arm so hard that it

hurt. I removed her fingers and held her hand instead.

There was a rustling from the bushes near us.

"The bear has a friend!" Myka said.

"We're under attack!" I shouted, my voice thick with fear.

The bushes shook, and I braced myself for the bear's BFF to jump out and eat us both.

"If this is the end," I told Myka, "you've been the best of friends to me, and I love you."

"Right back at you," she said.

"Hello? Bee? Myka? Everything okay?" a voice called out in the dark.

"Oh no! My dad! The bears are going to eat him!"

"What do we do?" Myka asked. "We need to stop him!"

But there wasn't any time. The only thing we could do was warn him.

"Dad! Stop! There are bears!" I yelled at the same time that Myka shined her flashlight on the table.

Two pairs of eyes were reflected in the light. Eyes hidden behind black masks.

"Raccoons!" Myka yelled, and burst out laughing. "It's not a bear! It's raccoons!"

The animals froze for a moment before they scurried off the table, taking our graham crackers with them.

"Nooooooo!" I wailed as they carried the graham crackers off into the darkness. "Not our s'mores supplies!"

"Girls, I thought I told you to clean everything up when you were done," Dad said in a stern voice.

"I thought we did," I said. "I must have missed some."

"Always double-check everywhere to make sure you put it all back into the SUV," Dad said, and I nodded. "Animals can get the tops off things, but they can't unlock cars. Lesson learned. At least it wasn't a bear."

I went over to the table and swept the graham cracker crumbs into my hand.

"What are you doing? The raccoons ate everything," Myka said.

"Cleaning up the crumbs," I told her. "We need to get rid of this. You never know when they might come back because they want *s'more*."

Myka and Dad groaned, but it was good to laugh after thinking we were going to be bear food.

The two of them joined me and helped clear off the table. Our all-you-can-eat buffet was now closed for business.

DON'T TAKE ME FOR PLANT-ED

Our first night might not have gone as planned, but I was determined to make the next day amazing. First up ... doughnuts and the sunrise!

Because who doesn't love doughnuts?

Apparently the rest of the Invincible Girls Club.

"Rise and shine!" I called to the group, using Dad's favorite morning greeting. Dad's favorite morning greeting. He had lent me his travel alarm, so I could get everyone up, but I appeared to be the only early riser. When no one stirred, I spoke a bit louder. "Wakey, wakey!"

Lauren groaned from deep within her sleeping bag.

"Up and at 'em! We don't want to be late! We have big plans to start the day," I said in an overly cheerful voice.

"The only thing I have planned is a few more hours of sleep," Emelyn grumbled.

"No can do," I said. "We need to go, or we'll be too late."

"Late for what?" Myka asked.

"The sunrise! Remember?" I asked. "I have breakfast, too; it's going to be great."

"Nothing sounds great this early," Emelyn said.

"Come on, this will be fun," I promised as I tickled Lauren to get her moving.

"Leave me alone," she said, and tried to swat at me with her arm.

"I have doughnuts," I told them, which I

thought would be sure to get them moving.

However, it did the opposite. Lauren burrowed deeper down into her sleeping bag, Emelyn didn't say anything, and Myka grumbled something that sounded like "good night."

"None of you want to go with me?" I asked, disappointment crushing my excitement.

When no one answered, I grabbed my knitting bag and crawled out of the tent. I wasn't going to force them to go.

"Hey, Bee," Dad said. He was at the picnic table, drinking from a mug and looking at his phone. "What's got you up so early?"

"Apparently nothing," I grumbled. "And I thought we agreed no technology."

He gave me a sheepish look. "Guilty as charged. I was checking in on your mom. Are the other girls still sleeping?"

"Unfortunately," I said.

"That doesn't sound good," he said.

"It isn't. I wanted to watch the sunrise, but no

one would wake up," I told him, and tried to keep the disappointment out of my voice.

"Well, as luck would have it, I'm up," Dad said, and grinned. "I'd love to watch the sunrise. We'll have to do it from here, though, since we can't leave the rest of the girls alone."

"The picnic table?" I moaned. "There's trees all over; we won't see anything."

"I'm sure we can find a patch where the sky is clear and watch it brighten. Listen to the birds and forest animals starting the day too. And bond, definitely bond," he said with a wink.

"Yeah, okay," I replied. It wasn't what I wanted, but he was right. I'd get to spend time with him.

"I need to get something from the car real quick," I told him, and raced over. It didn't take me long to grab what I was looking for.

"Is that what I think it is?" Dad asked as I headed back to the picnic table.

"I had Mom pick them up as a surprise for

this morning. Since you're the only one up, I guess we'll have to eat them together," I told Dad, and presented him with the box of doughnuts.

"Why do you make me do the hard stuff?" Dad joked.

It was still chilly out, so I had a blanket wrapped around me and these super-warm socks that Grammy had knitted. I cuddled up next to Dad after we had each picked out a doughnut.

"You know," Dad said, "when your mom and I first married and she worked the night shift at the hospital, I'd pick her up when she got off in the early morning, and the two of us would drink hot coffee and eat doughnuts in the parking lot as we watched the sun come up. Sunrise was kind of our thing."

"She doesn't work at night anymore," I said.

"Nope. After we had you, those long hours didn't seem important at all. What was important was you."

"So now the sunrise is our thing," I said, and gestured at the lightening sky.

"Perfect," Dad said. "Besides, once the baby comes, I'll probably already be up, since babies have no respect for night and day."

"Ugh, that means I'll be up too," I said.

"But you'll be an amazing big sister. No doubt the best in history," Dad said.

"It's not like I have a choice," I told him.

His voice turned serious. "I know your life has been flipped upside down and sharing a space isn't what you want to do. We'll figure it out."

"A tiny house in the backyard would be perfect for me. Then the baby can have its own room," I suggested, thinking about the show Grammy and I had watched where people built these teeny little places to live in.

"I'll build two . . . one for you and one for me!" Dad joked.

I picked up my knitting and thought about the possibilities as I added more rows to my

scarf. The sun started to brighten the sky, and it was nice to be there with Dad.

Until Dad pulled out his phone and scrolled through it. I cleared my throat, but he didn't get the message. I was about to say something when a way-too-familiar sound invaded the peace.

The sound of our neighbors singing.

The song.

The one and only song.

"It's too early for this," I groaned.

"At least it will get the other girls up. Relax.

We're having fun," Dad said, and glanced at his phone.

"What? You being on your phone? I thought we were spending time together. The idea was to get away from technology. You've been on that almost the entire time."

"Sorry, Bee. I've been checking in on your mom."

"But Grammy is right there," I said. "If Mom needs something, she can ask Grammy."

"I want your mom to know she can get in touch with me too if she needs anything," Dad reminded me.

I tried to hide my hurt, but it was hard. This getaway was for us, and here Dad was, attached to his phone because of Mom and the baby. I mean, I got why, but still.

Dad must have sensed that I was upset. "What about this? I can turn it to vibrate and only check it when I get a message. Would that help?"

"Big-time," I said.

"It's official. This phone will remain in my pocket while we hike, so you will get my one-hundred-percent-undivided attention. I'll be stuck to you like glue!"

I giggled. "I like the sound of that," I told Dad.

Then, as if they had been waiting for us to finish talking, our neighbors broke into another way-too-energizing song for that early in the morning. I covered my ears and groaned. "But that sound is a whole different story."

8 MAY THE FOREST BE WITH YOU

About an hour and a half later, my friends crawled out of the tent, blurry-eyed and rocking some hilarious bedhead.

"Finally," I said. "I didn't think you three would ever wake up."

"You missed a gorgeous sunrise," Dad said, and he was right. The sky had turned from pink to orange to red as the sun had risen. It was as if it had been putting on a show for us.

"We probably would've slept later if the singing hadn't started back up again," Emelyn complained.

"After the number of times we've heard it, I'm pretty sure I could perform that song with them," Myka said.

"Now that we're up, I have a very important question," Lauren said as she stretched. "What's for breakfast?"

"I'm not sure. My dad and I ate the doughnuts, because you sleepyheads didn't want to get up."

"Every single one?" Myka asked.

"You snooze, you lose," I said. "You should've joined us. I can probably find a granola bar or something for you."

"For real?" Lauren asked, disappointment on her face.

"Kidding. I figured we'd leave a few for when you finally decided to wake up." I held the box out to everyone. "Help yourself and fill up. We've got a long hike today. We leave in half an hour!"

"Half an hour? Are you sure? I didn't see you consult your agenda," Lauren said.

"I want to make it to the waterfall by lunchtime," I said, ignoring her. "It's supposed to be incredible, and a great spot to relax."

"I'm going to bring my sketchbook for sure," Emelyn said.

"I can use the binoculars that Carter lent me, to see if I can spot some birds!" Lauren added, mentioning her stepbrother.

"Maybe I'll do some sprints. No one said you can't stay in tip-top shape in the wild!" Myka declared as she flexed her arms.

I loved the excitement of my friends; I had finally done something right.

"Eat up. We need our energy!" I said, and shook the doughnut box at them. "When you're done, grab some water and pack your bags with anything else you need."

"Okay, boss!" Lauren said, and again the group

laughed, which stung a bit. I was only trying to be helpful.

After everyone ate, got dressed, and packed their book bags, we were ready to go.

"I've got the trail mix, so let's get on that trail!" I said, and thankfully, everyone simply cheered instead of laughing again at how prepared I was. Which was good for them—I had already decided that if they laughed, I wasn't going to share with anyone.

We fell into a gentle rhythm moving up the trail. Myka and I led the way with Dad bringing up the rear, while in the middle, Emelyn took pictures with her mom's camera of things she wanted to draw and Lauren scanned the woods with her binoculars, searching for birds and other animals.

Until things went downhill.

Literally.

"Oomph!" Lauren cried out when she tripped and fell over a root. Her binoculars flew out of her hand and slid down the trail. They picked up more and more momentum until they hit a rock and landed in a bush.

"Oh no!" Lauren wailed after I handed them back to her and she inspected them. "One of the lenses cracked. I had to promise Carter I'd take good care of them. He's going to be so mad."

"Accidents happen. I'm sure he'll understand," Dad said. "More important, are you okay?"

Lauren inspected her jeans, which were scraped up by the knees. "It hurts, but I don't see any blood."

"And now you have a cool pair of ripped

jeans," Emelyn pointed out, trying to look on the bright side.

"Thanks," Lauren said, and gave us a smile as she stood up and wiped the dirt off her pants.

The five of us continued our hike. We still had a ways to go, but we fueled up on trail mix.

Then disaster struck.

Again.

Emelyn got a blister.

At first she was still able to walk on it, but soon she could only limp up the trail.

"Maybe some Band-Aids," she told me. "I could

put a few over the blister and see if that works."

"Oh no," I said. I closed my eyes as disappointment in myself washed over me. I pictured the first-aid kit I had created, sitting in the glove compartment of Dad's car. I could see it as clear as day. I had put it there for easy access in case we needed it; I hadn't wanted anyone to have to search around for it in an emergency. A good idea—except when that emergency was toward the end of a three-mile hike on a trail that only went up from here.

"What's wrong?" Myka asked.

"I left the first-aid kit back at camp," I reluctantly admitted.

"Wait, what?" Lauren said. "Alert the press! Ruby, the world's best planner, forgot to bring Band-Aids."

Dad pretended to faint from shock, and Myka yelled, "Noooooooo! Whatever will we do?"

"Stop it," I said. They weren't funny. The situation wasn't funny. I'd spent so long planning this trip, and all anyone had been doing was laughing about that. Embarrassment from my mistake churned around inside me. "If you think the situation is so funny, see how you do on the trail alone. Because I'm done leading you."

In a blaze of anger, I took the map I had printed and ripped it into pieces. Tinier and tinier until it was nothing but confetti in my hands. I dropped it into my backpack, because maybe I was proving a point, but I wasn't about to litter.

Then I stomped away from everyone. Away from the trail, away from where the map told us to go, and away from their laughter.

"Bee, wait up!" Dad called, but I wasn't waiting. I was going. Far away from them.

CRACK!

There was a noise so loud, it seemed to shake everything around us.

"What in the world—" Myka started, but she

didn't have time to finish that sentence. Because before she could, the sky opened up and rain thundered down.

"Run for cover!" I shouted.

But with the map gone, I had no idea where to go to find cover.

So I ran.

And everyone followed me.

I took us farther up the trail and around a corner into the woods, where the trees were thicker. I hoped they'd be enough to shelter us from the rain. As we moved deeper in, they seemed to do the job. At least we weren't being drenched by the rain. We huddled together and watched as the clouds moved out almost as quickly as they'd moved in, blue sky pushing its way back.

"Well, that certainly was a surprise," Dad said once the storm had passed.

"Maybe we should skip the rest of the hike and get into some dry clothes," Myka said. "I'm soaked."

Lauren hugged herself and nodded. "It's cold out here."

They were right; the storm had cooled everything down. I was ready to go back to our campsite too, but there was a tiny problem.

Without the map, I had absolutely no idea where we were or how to get back.

The Invincible Girls Club was officially lost.

WOOD YOU BELIEVE WE'RE LOST?

I sank down and sat on the wet ground with my face in my hands.

What in the world were we going to do?

I had messed everything up, and now we might never get out of the woods.

Someone put their hand on my back and said my name in a soft voice.

"Ruby," Emelyn repeated. "I'm sorry we laughed at you."

"Yeah, thank you so much. We appreciate

everything you've planned for this trip," Myka said, which made me feel a million times worse because there had been so much that had gone wrong that I hadn't planned for.

I sniffled and shook my head.

"It's not that," I said to the four of them. "I mean, yeah, it's awful when you laugh at me, but we have bigger problems now."

They stood around me, warmth and concern on their faces.

"How can we help?" Emelyn asked, but it was a hopeless kind of question. There was nothing she could do. There was nothing anyone could do. I'd had the map, and now I didn't. It was gone and so was our way home.

Grammy always said there was nothing more important than speaking your truth, but what happened when the truth would make everyone mad at you?

But it was *not* speaking the truth that had gotten me into this whole mess. If I had told

everyone from the start how I felt about them laughing at my plans and schedules, I never would've torn up the map and stormed away.

I took a deep breath before speaking again. "We're officially lost."

"Lost?" Lauren asked.

"The way was easy when we were on the trail, but since we ran to find shelter from the rain,

I have no idea where we are now." I waved my hand around the woods. "I have no idea where we are, and I tore up the map. We could be anywhere."

"I'm sure it's not that big a deal," Emelyn said.

"At this point I don't even know up from down," I confessed.

Myka looked around for a moment, deep in thought. "The GPS! On your dad's phone. We can use it for directions!"

"That's a great plan!" I said, and turned to Dad. "Can we try that?"

Dad doubled over in laughter. "Oh, so *now* you're okay with me pulling out my phone?"

"Desperate times call for desperate measures," I joked. "Including using technology on a technology-free weekend."

Dad pulled out his phone, swiped at the screen with his finger, and frowned. He wiped the phone against his shorts and swiped again.

"Everything okay?" I asked.

"The rain," he said. "It must have gotten my phone wet."

My shoulders sagged. I didn't have to ask to know what he'd say next.

"It's not working," he said, and let out a loud sigh.

"At all?" Emelyn asked.

"At all," Dad confirmed. "But don't worry, we'll find our way back to our campsite."

"There's only two ways we can go," Myka said. "Up or down."

"We don't even know where the trail is," I told them.

"Life doesn't always need a map. Sometimes the best surprises happen when they aren't planned," Dad said.

"Yes! Like when we volunteered at the dog shelter," Lauren said. "Pretty sure we never expected to get a ton of dogs adopted."

"You're right," I said. "It's just that life seems so chaotic and messy right now, it helps me if I can know what's going to happen."

"In other words, you like to be in control?" Lauren said.

"Someone has to be," I said. "Especially when some of you don't plan at all."

"Hey, I like surprises!" Lauren joked.

"That's why we make an incredible team," Emelyn added. "What one of us doesn't have, the others do."

"And when our forces join, we are invincible!" Myka said, and pumped her fist in the air.

"Maybe you're right," I said, and the words did feel true. Maybe I didn't always need to control things. Maybe I should let things go and see what happened.

Except right then wasn't exactly the best time to do that. Right then we needed to figure out how to get back to our campground.

"Maybe we should try to find a trail first," Lauren suggested, which made sense. "I'm just not sure which way we should head."

"That way," I said, and pointed toward my left.

"That's the right direction?" Dad asked.

I shrugged. "I have no idea, but you're the one who told me to embrace surprises. This can be the first one . . . discovering if this is the way back."

"Let's go," Lauren said, and headed in the direction I had pointed.

We walked through the overgrowth and pushed away branches of leaves for about five minutes as the forest got denser. I wanted to speak up and tell her that this might not be the best choice, but I told myself to let it go, to see what happened, which was exactly what I did.

But after a while, it was obvious we weren't finding our way out of the woods. We were headed deeper into it.

"Maybe this wasn't the right way," I offered.

The group paused and we looked around us.

"Where do bears go when it rains?" Emelyn asked.

"There aren't any bears here," I told her, and repeated Dad's words. "They don't want anything to do with us."

My friends stared at me, unconvinced.

"I'm scared," Emelyn whispered, saying out loud what we had all been thinking deep down inside.

"Me too," Lauren agreed.

"It's going to be all right," Dad said, but his voice didn't sound as confident as I wanted it to be.

That was when we heard it.

A noise I was way too familiar with.

I held my finger to my lips to silence everyone.

The noise was louder this time. Closer.

Myka's eyes grew wide. "Is that what I think it is?"

We stood still and waited. When the noise happened again, I began to laugh from relief.

"It's the most beautiful song in the world!" I confirmed.

And it truly was. Because what I heard was our campsite neighbors singing their hearts out as they went on their own hike. This time, when the song started again, it was music to my ears.

It was funny how things could flip so quickly, and what you once hated could become the best thing in the world.

"We need to get their attention before it's too late," I said.

"We can follow them back!" Myka said, realization dawning in her mind.

"Exactly! They probably even have a map," I said. "I mean, if you're cool with a map."

"A map sounds perfect. I've had enough surprises today," Lauren said.

"Follow that music!" I said, and we raced toward the voices, ready for their song to lead us home.

I CAMP BELIEVE OUR LUCK!

It turned out our neighbors—Katherine, Zara, and Donovan—had an incredible story of their own. One we never would've known if they hadn't led us back to camp.

"Can you believe they're in a real live band? One with albums, concerts, and fans?" Myka said as we sat around the campfire that night. It was true. They were in a band called Enchanted Forest and toured all over. They were working on a third album and had gone camping for inspiration.

"It's the best way to write new music because there are no distractions," Zara had said as they'd led us back to camp.

"I hope our singing didn't bother you," Katherine had added.

"Bother us? Not at all," I'd said, and ignored the smirks from my friends.

"Sometimes we get into the zone and can't stop until we get the song just right," Zara had explained.

10

"We'd love to try out our new stuff on you," Donovan had said. "Get some feedback. Any interest in joining us for a campfire tonight?"

I'd turned to Dad. "Can we? Please?"

"I don't see why not," Dad had said. "Especially since you've been such a fan of their music this weekend."

"A big fan," I'd agreed, and shared a knowing look with Dad.

The funny thing was that, as we sat there listening to the band sing at their campfire, I really *was* a fan.

"Do you know what's even cooler than running into rock stars in the woods?" Lauren asked as she toasted a marshmallow on the fire.

"What?" I asked.

She held up a giant chocolate bar. "That they remembered to bring *all* the ingredients for s'mores."

"Ha ha ha," I said, but I didn't take it personally. I was over letting every little thing bother me.

"The joke is on you, because when I get home, I still have a mound of chocolate bars just for me."

"Or a future camping trip!" Myka suggested. "I'm officially hooked!"

"Me too!" Emelyn said, and Lauren nodded in agreement.

"That's a great idea!" I agreed. "This trip turned out to be everything I needed."

"Everything we *all* needed!" Myka said.

Well, almost, I thought. There was one last thing I had to take care of.

"I'll be back," I said, and stood up.

Dad sat at our neighbor's picnic table a few feet away from us and bobbed his head to the beat of a song Enchanted Forest was singing. He had said he wanted to give us girls time to hang out, but I was pretty sure he just wanted a break from our nonstop talking. He nodded toward the bench he sat on.

"How's my best girl doing?" he asked when I settled down next to him.

"Good," I said, but then paused. "Well, almost.

There's something I need to talk to you about."

Dad leaned back against the table. "This sounds serious."

"It kind of is," I said. "I wanted to tell you the other reason why I wanted to go on this trip and why I was upset about you spending time on the phone."

Dad raised an eyebrow. "The other reason? It wasn't about getting away from it all and bonding?"

"It was," I said. "But there's more to it. You and Mom have been obsessed with getting ready for the new baby that it seems as if you don't have room for anything or anyone else. And I'm worried."

"Worried? About what?" Dad asked in a voice that sounded so kind and concerned that it was easy to say the next part.

"You and Mom forgetting about me," I said.

"Oh, Bee," Dad said. "We would never, ever, ever forget about you."

"Lately it's felt that way," I told him.

"Things have been really busy," Dad said, and

he paused, lost in thought. "I'm glad you said something, because you're right. This weekend has reminded me of how much I love to spend time with you. Something I haven't done often lately. We've been super focused on the baby and that hasn't been fair to you."

"Wait, I'm right?" I asked, surprised.

"Completely right."

"Pretty soon things are going to change and our family will be different," I said.

"It might seem that way at first. Babies demand a lot of attention, but you'll always be my Bee. I've got a big heart. I can fit all of you in here." Dad patted his stomach. "See, nice and big."

"I think you've got your body parts mixed up," I said through giggles.

"Nope, my heart is so big that it's pushing out my stomach."

"Interesting," I said. "You learn something new every day."

"And today I want you to learn that your part

in our family is never going to change. Your mom and I love you very much, and your new little brother or sister will be so incredibly blessed to have you in their life."

"You think?" I asked.

"I know," Dad said. "You're something special, Bee. Seriously, how did I get so lucky?"

"How did I get so lucky to have you?" I asked back.

"We might be the two luckiest people in the entire world!" Dad declared, which at that moment seemed pretty true.

As I sat there with him, watching my friends talk and laugh around the fire, I understood that there were some things you couldn't plan, control, or schedule.

Like the love you had for another person.

Especially a new baby sibling you hadn't even met yet.

Love just happened.

And your heart always made room.

THE BEST THINGS IN LIFE ARE TREE

11

"**W**akey, wakey," a voice said, pulling me from a dream.

"Rise and shine," someone else said, and pointed a flashlight at me.

It took me a few seconds to realize where I was and that my friends were saying the exact same things I had said to them the morning before.

Lauren even tickled me until I got out of my sleeping bag.

Emelyn held my shoes out to me.

"Put these on," she said. "And a sweatshirt. We have to get moving."

"What's going on?" I asked, still groggy from sleep.

"We're going to watch the sunrise," Myka announced. "All four of us!"

"For real?" I asked. A rush of love filled me, and I grinned at my friends.

"Someone told us that it was something we had to do, and I didn't want to let that moment pass," Myka said.

"You're the best," I said.

"We need to get moving or we'll miss the sunrise," Emelyn reminded us.

"Sounds like someone else is seeing the importance of a schedule," I joked as I crawled out of the tent.

Dad sat at the picnic table with a mug of coffee and a book open in his lap.

"You're up too?" I asked.

"Wouldn't miss it! I'm going to walk to the

lake with you so you can see the sunrise there," he said, and held up the book. "Don't worry, I'll give you girls some privacy and promise not to get you lost."

"After what happened yesterday, that's a big promise," I said.

"Not anymore!" He stood and pulled his phone out of his pocket. The screen lit up when he turned it toward me.

"It works!" I said.

"Yep! Must have dried out. But I'll only bring it just in case," he said as he slipped it back into his pocket. "I forgot how nice it is to sit and read a good book."

"See!" I said. "Getting away from it all is a good thing!"

"Then let's get moving away from our camp-ground," Lauren said, and made a sweeping motion with her hands to get us going.

We headed toward the lake, which was a ten-minute walk. We used our flashlights on the path. The sky was still holding on to the night.

Once we got there, Emelyn spread out a blanket near the edge of the shore and we huddled under another two blankets that we draped over our shoulders.

"Sorry things started a bit rocky," I told my friends.

"No big deal," Emelyn said. "We had fun."

"I think maybe I needed some of that stuff to happen to realize that sometimes the best

moments are the ones you don't plan for," I confessed.

"It's true! Getting lost was a win for us," Emelyn said. "We met rock stars!"

"Rock stars who agreed to let me write an article about them for our school paper," I added, giddy at the idea. Katherine, Zara, and Donovan had given me their phone numbers and promised an interview.

"I have some new supercool ripped jeans from my fall," Lauren joked.

"And after all the time we spent both on and off the trail, I've learned that hiking is great conditioning for sports. I'm seeing a family hike in my future," Myka said.

"Maybe schedules really are overrated," I said. "Our best moments this weekend came from stuff we hadn't planned."

"Speaking of schedules, what are we up to today?" Emelyn asked.

I pictured the page in my notebook. The one

I had spent so much time working on before we had left for this trip. The one I had packed full of activities. Then I pictured the next page. The blank one I hadn't written on yet.

"Absolutely nothing," I said, and I loved the sound of that.

The sound of possibility.

The sound of surprise.

The sound of four Invincible Girls ready to start a day where anything could happen.

LAUGH S'MORE, WORRY LESS

The first thing I did when Dad and I got home was find Mom and wrap my arms around her in a giant hug.

"Whoa, easy there," she said, but held tight to me. "Remember, you're hugging two of us."

"I missed you both," I told her.

"You can't even imagine how much I missed you," Mom said, and pushed some of my hair off my face.

"And you can't imagine how much I missed my coffee maker and warm showers," Dad declared. "As a matter of fact, I call dibs on the bathroom."

"Tell me all about it," Mom said as she pulled me onto the couch beside her. I filled her in. Everything that we had done . . . the good, the bad, the surprising, and amazing.

"What about you?" I asked. "How was your weekend? Did you get to relax?"

"Quite the opposite. I've been very busy." Her eyes lit up with a mischievous look. "I've been doing a little bit of redecorating."

"The house looks the same as it always has," I told her.

She gave me another sneaky look and shrugged. "Go check out your room; I think you're going to like what we've done to the place."

"My room?" I asked. "We?"

"Grammy and me. I realized that we were doing it all wrong. We only focused on what the baby needed. We didn't think about what you needed. So that's what Grammy and I set out to do while you were away."

I followed Mom to my room. She paused before pushing open the door.

"I hope you like it," she said nervously.

"I'm sure I'll love it," I told her, to be nice, but inside I was worried. What had she done to my room? With everything else changing, I wasn't sure I could handle my safe, familiar room being different too.

I slowly opened the door and was surprised to see a fully built changing table, crib, and rocking chair. There were even pictures of baby animals hanging on the wall. It was an adorable nursery for a baby.

"What is that?" I pointed at two giant pieces of fabric that hung from the ceiling to the floor, parallel to the door. They each stretched across half the room and met in the middle to form an opening. The fabric was a pale blue color. The sun shone through the window and made it almost glow, like the sky. The sky on our camping trip.

"Your wall," Mom said.

"My wall?"

"Yep, check it out. You can enter through the middle."

"Enter what?" I asked.

Mom threw up her hands. "For goodness' sake, Ruby! Stop asking all these questions and find out for yourself!"

She pushed me toward the curtain. I grabbed the middle section where it was separated and stepped through it to the other half of my room. A miniature version of my room. Everything was in the same position, and the fabric curtain made it feel as if it were a separate room. Not only that, but the ceiling was covered with small glow-in-the-dark stars. Tons of them all over.

"This really is like the sky at our campsite," I breathed, as the sun made pale blue waves on the wall and ceiling through the fabric.

"I wanted you to remember your trip, and Dad mentioned in one of his texts how you loved how many stars there were," Mom said. "Now you can see them every night."

"It's magical," I said.

"I know it isn't easy to give up your room, especially when it's for a baby. Privacy is important. Since we couldn't add to the house, I thought this was the next best thing."

I couldn't believe Mom and Grammy had done this for me. "It's perfect. Thank you so much!"

Mom flashed me another sneaky grin. "That's not your only surprise, though. There's another project Grammy and I worked on, but we have to go to her apartment for it."

I hadn't seen Grammy yet, so I was excited and anxious to tell her about our adventures.

We waited for Dad to finish his shower.

"Did you know about this?" I asked him as we headed downstairs.

"I sure did. Why do you think I was on the phone that first morning?"

"Wait, that was about the surprise?"

"Your mom had some questions and things I needed to walk them through," Dad said.

"Not that many," Mom interrupted with a grin. "I followed the instructions, unlike some people, who think they can do it without them."

"I can't believe that's what you were talking about," I said.

"We thought of it the other day," Dad said. "Your mom was so excited about it all."

"You're the best," I told the two of them.

"There she is, the greatest outdoorsman in the world," Grammy said as I walked through her door.

"Don't you mean 'outdoors*woman*'?" I corrected her. "And I can guarantee you that I'm not the greatest in the world. After you hear about our weekend, you'll instantly take back that title."

"But did you have fun?" Grammy asked.

"So much fun!" I said.

"Then that's what matters," she said, and pointed toward what she called her junk room. Grammy was notorious for everything she held on to, and my parents were always trying to talk her into clearing up the space. "I really hope what I have for you behind that door was worth the time your mom and I put into it this weekend."

I stepped inside, and instead of the piles and piles of Grammy's stuff, the room was clean and had a desk and a bed. There was a cabinet filled with yarn, and a tiny TV in the corner.

"What is all this?" I asked.

"I call it the Ruby Retreat!" she announced, and continued to talk when she saw my confusion. "This is officially your room to come hang out in or escape to whenever you need to. We created a pretty cool area for you in your room, but there will be times when you need more than that."

"This is really for me?" I asked.

"It sure is! Your mom and I had a lot of fun

creating it. You're always welcome to stay here."

"Even in the middle of the night?" I joked.

"Especially in the middle of the night," Grammy said. "I know how babies can be."

We laughed, and I looked at the room again, not believing this was for me.

"I left this weekend thinking I didn't have a place of my own at all here, and now I have two!"

Dad cleared his throat. "There's also something else we wanted to talk to you about. I know you hated that I was on my phone this weekend, and I admit, it was nice to put it down and out of sight, but sometimes technology isn't a bad thing."

Mom held a gift-wrapped present out to me.

"A gift?" I asked, confused.

"Open it, big sister," Mom said.

I unwrapped the gift, and inside was a black-and-white printout in a frame.

"What is this?" I asked.

"This, my sweet Ruby, is one of the first pictures of your new baby sister," Mom said, and placed her hand on her bump.

"My new sister?" I asked, and realization settled inside me. "Wait! You're having a girl?"

"We sure are!" Dad said, and my parents grinned.

"A new member of our club!" I said as I stared at the printout of the sonogram. I placed it on the desk next to the bed and sat in the super-comfy armchair next to the window. "I can't wait to show her how to be an Invincible Girl!"

"She'll learn from the best," Mom said.

"Thanks," I said. "I'm sorry if I gave you both a hard time about feeling left out."

"I'm glad you said something," Dad said. "You'll *always* belong here or wherever else we may end up."

It was then I noticed that the shaky feeling inside was gone. Instead it had been replaced with something warm, and cozy, and full of love. The feeling of being home.

I opened my knitting bag and pulled out my scarf.

Grammy pointed at it. "You're almost done!"

"I thought I was," I told her. I held it up so she could see the whole thing. I had worked on it in the car and around the campfire, and it had gotten a bit longer. There wasn't much more to do, but that didn't matter. I had other plans for the yarn now. I pulled the stitches off the needle and began to unravel the yarn.

"What are you doing? Fixing a mistake?" Grammy asked.

"Nope. I realized the yarn is destined for another purpose," I told her. "I'm taking a break from scarves."

"Wow, you really are a changed girl," Grammy joked. "What are you going to make instead?"

"A blanket for my new sister," I said, and at that moment, I felt so much love in the room that I thought I might burst from happiness.

Grammy clapped her hands in delight. "That's the perfect project!" she said, and I couldn't have agreed more.

It was perfect.

This all was.

Absolutely positively magnificently perfect.

Hello, Amazing Reader!

This book is especially near and dear to my heart because, unlike in the other books, the girls don't do something big or grand. They don't help a large group of people or animals. They don't change the world in a huge way. Instead this book celebrates friendship and nature and the peace the natural world can bring people.

I was a camper and then a counselor at an overnight summer camp for fourteen years and loved every moment of it. There was something so magical about the land. All I had to do was step onto the campground, and a calm would wash over me. I still carry those memories with me over twenty years later and keep in touch with many of the friends I made while there. My son will soon be a camper there for the first time, and

I hope he finds the same connection with nature that I did.

If life ever feels too busy or too fast, step outside and take a deep breath. Watch the clouds move past in the sky, go on a hike, or count the stars. Take a moment to slow life down and remember how invincible the world and you can be in those quiet, simple moments.

Love,

Rachele Alpine

aka . . . a lifetime member of the Invincible Girls Club

MEET
INVINCIBLE GIRL
Cheryl Strayed

When Cheryl Strayed was twenty-six, she set out to hike the Pacific Crest Trail. She had gone through some loss in her life and looked toward nature as a way to help her heal. However, she had never hiked before. She didn't let that stop her, though! Cheryl hiked eleven hundred miles alone during the course of three months and faced obstacles such as snow, getting lost, and having shoes that didn't fit and injured her feet. Cheryl is an Invincible Girl because through her time spent hiking the trail, she understood how powerful nature can be and used its gifts to help her understand how strong she can truly be.

MEET
INVINCIBLE GIRL
Tasha Tudor

Tasha Tudor was enamored with the natural world. From a young age she surrounded herself with everything that nature, animals, and simple living offered. She was a popular children's book author and illustrator. She wrote and illustrated twenty-four books, and her art has appeared in more than one hundred texts. She often painted the landscapes that surrounded her in New England towns, and the lives of animals in their natural setting. She lived a life free of modern conveniences, instead knitting her own sweaters, making her own clothes, and raising animals on a farm. She even lived without electricity for the first five years of her son's life! Tasha was an Invincible Girl because she used her artistic talents to share the wonders and magic of the world around her with others.

MEET
INVINCIBLE GIRL
Woniya Thibeault

Woniya Thibeault is devoted to living life off the grid, being dependent entirely on herself, and using only what nature has provided. She gathers her food, makes her clothes, and lives a life away from modern society. She even lived on her own in a remote location, where she could bring only ten items, for seventy-three days. Woniya started a movement called Buckskin Revolution that invites others to learn her "wilderness living" skills and empower themselves to live a life like their ancestors, using nature's gifts. Woniya is an Invincible Girl because she shows people the power they have within themselves to live without material items.

MEET
INVINCIBLE GIRL
Elizabeth Gilbert

Elizabeth Gilbert used traveling the world as her teacher to find peace in her life. She experienced the country of Italy through the food it provided, India through prayer and meditation, and Bali by finding new forms of love, including loving and accepting herself for who she is, flaws and all. Elizabeth is an Invincible Girl because she embraces all that the world and its people have to offer, in order to grow and discover who she really is.

INVINCIBLE GIRL
Danielle Williams

Danielle Williams lives for adventure. She fell in love with it while in the army after she did her first jump from a plane. Since that moment, she's done over six hundred more jumps out of planes. Danielle cofounded Team Blackstar, which is a group of Black skydivers from around the world who connect to do jumps. However, she quickly saw that there was a need to create an even bigger network to promote the love of all things outdoors for Black people, Indigenous peoples, and other people of color. She created Melanin Base Camp, with the focus of increasing representation in media and advertisements of all people in the outdoors. Danielle is an Invincible Girl because her efforts have opened up the world of the outdoors to those who might not have seen themselves there before. She's shown the world that everyone belongs.

MEET
INVINCIBLE GIRL
Juliette Gordon Low

Juliette, called Daisy by family and friends, was always looking for her next adventure. Although she became deaf when she was twenty-six, she never let that stop her. She formed a club called the Helping Hands. She spent much of her time as an adult making art and doing charity work. After the death of her husband, Juliette founded the Girl Scouts, an organization that is still popular today. Juliette was an Invincible Girl because she showed the world what girls can do when they come together and work for the good of everyone around them.

INVINCIBLE GIRL
Candice English

Candice English celebrates her ancestry and home state of Montana in one of Ruby's favorite ways . . . she dyes yarns! She mixes her love of the land and fiber arts together to create colorways that are inspired by the landscapes around her. Her color combinations also pay tribute to her

Blackfeet heritage as she draws on language and legends. As Candice's business grew, she knew she wanted to help other Indigenous communities in Montana, so she started the nonprofit Sisters United. This organization provides support to women, children, and communities throughout Montana to help preserve their culture and provide safety. Candice is an Invincible Girl because through color and art she honors the land she inhabits, making it a priority to give back and preserve the land's history.

INVINCIBLE GIRL
Mary Oliver

Mary Oliver loved nature since she was a young child. She would often spend the day in the woods near her house when she needed to get away. She loved the peace and calm the natural world would provide and found herself writing poetry inspired by the time she spent outside. Mary lived a very simple life, more interested in the animals and land around her than material goods. She went on long walks and used nature as a source of creation. Mary was an Invincible Girl because she slowed down her life to appreciate the world around her and wrote poems as an homage.

MEET
INVINCIBLE GIRL
Robin Wall Kimmerer

Dr. Robin Wall Kimmerer is both a scientist and a nature writer. She is a huge advocate for the earth and her Indigenous background, and often connects the two. She wrote *Gathering Moss* and *Braiding Sweetgrass*, a book that combines her knowledge as an Indigenous woman with scientific facts, in order to provide an understanding of the environment and the world around her. Robin is an Invincible Girl because of her respect for her ancestry and for science.

INVINCIBLE GIRL
Angelou Ezeilo

Angelou was raised in urban New Jersey. However, every summer she would go to upstate New York and spend time in the open space and natural world. Angelou remembered those summers and how they helped spark an appreciation of the land and conservation. She wanted others to see that connection, as a way to encourage them to create a life focused on the environment and sustainability. She created Greening Youth Foundation, a nonprofit that provides education, opportunities, and experiences for under-represented and diverse youths, allowing them to spend time in the outdoors and learn about how to make a difference in the earth's future. Angelou is an Invincible Girl because she has introduced thousands of kids and young adults to the outdoors and inspired them to see the importance of treating our earth with respect and care.

MEET
INVINCIBLE GIRL
Elizabeth Duvivier

Elizabeth is a creative spirit through and through. She's a talented author, artist, teacher, yogi, and champion for others. She spends much of her time outdoors, enjoying the beauty and simplicity of nature. Elizabeth is a huge advocate for marginalized artists, and works to elevate their voices and art. She created a retreat called Squam, which invites people from all over the world to leave their busy lives behind and spend time immersed in nature, connecting with themselves and others through creativity. She uses the environment as a way to teach people how to slow down and see the gifts that our earth can offer. Elizabeth is an Invincible Girl because of her dedication to showing everyone how a life of creativity can bring magic and joy.

Ways That You Can Be an Invincible Girl and Celebrate the Magic of Nature and Simple Living!

🌿 Go camping! This can be done by actually getting away and going into the woods, or by just pitching a tent in your backyard!

🌿 Have a technology-free day once a week when you and your family don't use the TV, phones, computers, video games, or other items that can distract you rather than bring you together.

🌿 Buy or make a bird feeder and hang it somewhere you can watch the birds come. If you're artistic (like Emelyn), consider drawing the ones that visit!

🌿 Start a nature journal. Spend time each day reflecting on the world around you and writing down observations.

- Create a nature scavenger hunt. Make a list of items found in nature (such as a flower, leaf, bee, blue jay . . .) and then see what you can find! Each time you spot one of these items, cross them off your list.
- Build a campfire and tell stories. (Don't forget the marshmallows *and* chocolate!)
- Go on a hike! Explore new places around you and discover what nature has to offer.
- Adopt some land: find land that you can go to often, and make it your mission to keep it clean, free of litter, and a place for other people to enjoy.
- Have a s'mores-making competition. Who can create the best flavor combination? (My favorite is marshmallows and peanut butter cups!) Make sure to taste all the entries!
- Research recipes and make something over the fire. (You could even try Ruby's awesome baked potatoes!)

- Find a spot in your house just for you. Make it your special place where you can get away when you need time to yourself.

- Take up knitting, like Ruby did. It's a great meditative activity to help relax and clear your mind. Make items that you can donate to others or give as surprise gifts to friends and family members. Hats and scarves are quick knits that can then be donated to homeless shelters.

- Start a gratitude journal. Each day before you go to bed, add items that you're thankful for.

- Go on a night hike with your family. Use a flashlight, but turn it off to count the stars in the sky.

- Watch the sunrise or sunset. (You can even bring doughnuts!)

- Knit a weather scarf: Designate a color for each temperature range. For example, 90–100 degrees could be red, 80–89 could be pink,

70–79 could be yellow. Then knit a row each day, corresponding to the temperature outside. After a year you'll have a scarf showing the weather each day!

🌿 Learn how to identify stars in the sky. Spend an evening stargazing.

🌿 Make a fairy garden in your yard, or in the woods for someone else to find.

🌿 Learn camping skills—how to build a fire, how to pitch a tent, how to navigate with a compass, how to read the stars in the sky.